House-Sitter Virgin

A First Time with Her Brother's Best Friend Steamy Short Romance

Kandie Kissimmie

For Adults Only – This short story includes sensual descriptions of erotic sexual situations. All characters in it are represented as 18 or older and are not related. It is intended only for adults over the age of 18.

The following tropes appear in this book: sweet & spicy, brother's best friend, first time, age gap, steamy scene in the pool, short story

CONTENTS

CHAPTER 1 - ADRIANA

The hardwood floors are cool under my feet as I walk into the kitchen and mix up a cocktail for a late afternoon outside at the pool.

"Don't forget, I'm working a double, so I'm crashing at home before coming back over tomorrow afternoon."

"K," I say as I wave to my best friend, Bella, as she leaves for her summer job at the diner.

Being on summer break, Bella and I jumped on the chance to house-sit for my brother, Adam, and his roommate, Rowan. It just so happened that both of them had out-of-town conferences this week for work, although funnily enough, on opposite sides of the country.

It's a luxurious house they're subletting from Adam's boss who is living abroad for an unknown period. The two-story stucco is in a gated community with a private entrance from the street and an in-ground pool in the backyard.

I'm just getting ready to head out back to the pool when the doorbell rings. I put my pina colada down in the kitchen and answer it to find a package. When I pick it up, I see my online order has arrived early. *Yay!*

Excited to try it on, I run to the guest room and rip the package open. It's cream colored, bringing out my tan, and fits me perfectly. I'm kind of busty, and the top creates beautiful cleavage. The bottoms are high cut and more of a thong in the back than I expected. I'm thankful Bella and I recently had a spa day, and both got Brazilians.

I pull my long, blonde hair out of my ponytail, shaking it out so it hangs down in waves down my back, and check myself out one more time in the mirror. It's super cute, and it's really too bad nobody is going to see me in it today. I'm sure Mr. Todd, the old man next door, would love to have a peek. But a privacy fence surrounds the backyard. Thank goodness.

Truthfully, I'd purchased the bathing suit in hopes of Rowan seeing me wearing it. I imagine what he might think of it and my heart races and a warmth spreads through my body like wildfire. My brother Adam had always been overprotective, his friends too afraid to even look in my direction since I was his little sister. But I never really paid any attention to them anyway... until Rowan came along.

Adam and Rowan had been close friends since college; then just last year they both got jobs back in our hometown and ended up renting this house together. But I hadn't ever met Rowan until a year ago. When I first saw him, I thought my heart was going to beat right out of my chest.

I grab my pina colada and head out to the pool. Then, streaming a radio station to the outdoor speaker, I lie down on the pool float and place my drink on the side of the pool.

I've only been outside for fifteen minutes when I hear a deep voice. "You shouldn't be out here all alone, especially if you're drinking."

I jump, startled, and fall off the float into the water. I look up to see Rowan standing there, grinning. His eyes crinkle at the corners and the wind ruffles his dark hair.

Rowan chuckles. The asshole.

"Rowan!" I scold him. "You scared the shit out of me."

He holds his hand down to me. "Sorry. I'll help you out."

I grab his hand and tug just enough, so he loses his balance and topples into the pool with me. He comes up out of the water soaking wet, his polo stuck to his perfect physique that's cut like a statue.

I smirk. "Karma's a bitch."

He grins and shakes his head, pulling himself up and out of the water. I decide to use the ladder. Rowan grabs a towel from the basket and hands me one, then towels himself off.

"What are you doing home?" I ask. Suddenly realizing my luck. I'm going to be here alone with Rowan. And I'm wearing my new bikini.

He shrugs. "Trip got cut short."

"Well, in that case, you should go change into something more appropriate for the pool."

He goes inside and returns wearing swim trunks. I try not to stare too much at his tan abs, but dear god, they're like a washboard.

We hang out by the pool for a bit, reclining in the lounge chairs. Our conversation flows effortlessly as he tells me about his recent work trip to L.A. and I tell him about my college plans.

Eventually, he orders takeout for us and has it delivered to the house. We eat spicy shrimp linguine ala vodka and warm breadsticks out on the patio and share a bottle of wine.

As we eat and talk, I feel his gaze lingering on my curves. I don't dare change out of my bikini, not just yet, anyway. I want to savor this moment, this feeling of being carefree and beautiful in his eyes.

The sun slowly dips behind the horizon, painting the sky a brilliant shade of orange and pink. The stars twinkle in the navy night sky as Rowan dives into the pool with a splash.

"Come join me!" He beckons, laughing.

I hesitate for a moment before jumping into the water. Suddenly, a slow song plays on the radio.

Rowan grabs my hands and smiles mischievously, pulling me towards him. "Come dance with me," he says. I laugh and glance around. "In the pool?"

He shrugs good-naturedly. "Why not?"

His firm hands circle my waist, sending a chorus of electric sparks up my spine as he draws me closer. I tremble against his chest, my body quivering with anticipation. We move in unison among the gentle ripples of water, and I am overwhelmed with a woodsy aroma that reminds me of fresh cedar mixed with a hint of citrus. I feel intoxicated by his presence, captivated by his scent, like an aphrodisiac.

Our bodies move together as if they were made for each other, and all I can think about is how much I want to kiss him. His lips are so close that all I have to do is lean up just a little bit and they'll be against mine. So, I do it, my eyes closing as my lips meet his with a gentle pressure.

We kiss softly at first, exploring each other slowly. Then our tongues dart playfully against one another, and our hands explore each other's body hungrily.

My bikini top has come undone somewhere along the way, leaving my breasts exposed to

Rowan's touch. He cups them gently in his hands, sending sparks of pleasure through my body.

He takes my bottom lip between his teeth as he presses his body against mine. It feels like paradise as we drift further into the depths of this passionate embrace. Every inch of me is alive; every nerve on fire with desire for this man before me. We continue kissing until finally we part, both gasping for air and trying to understand what just happened between us.

His eyes search my face, dark and full of desire. "I want you, Adriana." He takes a step back and shakes his head. "I thought I could do this but ..." his voice trails off.

The water laps against my bare skin, and I feel the heat of his gaze on my body. My nipples pucker in the cool air, and I cross my arms. "But what Rowan?"

"I'm worried you'll regret it." He finally says.

My heart races as I move toward Rowan, my hand trembles as I reach up to cup his face in my hands.

"Rowan," I whisper nervously. "I'm a big girl. It's just sex, right? No strings attached." But deep down, I know that isn't true. I want more than his body; I am hoping for something so much deeper.

He runs his hand through his wet hair, droplets running down his face and neck until they disappear into the pool. "Yeah, with my best friend's little sister." He hesitates before adding, "Who is off limits."

I shake my head vehemently. "Adam doesn't own my body," I say firmly. "He can't dictate who I sleep with or anything else about my life."

He still doesn't look convinced, but when he speaks again, there is an underlying vulnerability in his voice. "But are you sure? You're still a virgin... right?" he asks, barely more than a whisper.

I groan, annoyance bubbling up within me. "God! Does everyone know? Does my brother just go around telling everyone every little detail of my life?"

His expression softens, and he reaches out and grabs my hand. His grip is sure and warm as he asks one final question. "You really want me to be the one?"

My head bobs slowly, my eyes never leaving his.

He lifts an eyebrow in surprise, as if he hadn't expected that answer. "Why?" He asks.

I roll my eyes and absently run my finger along the back of his hand. "Well, other than the fact that you are hot as fuck," I say with a smirk, "I trust you."

His lips curve up in amusement. "You think I'm hot as fuck?"

"Come here," I say before leaning in to kiss him again. This time it's even more intense than before; more urgent and desperate, as if he needs this too.

We kiss deeper and harder. His hands playing with my breasts. He lifts me up so my legs wrap around him, and I can feel his rock-hard cock pressing against me. I wrap my legs tighter around him and move my hips, trying to get more friction while he palms my ass cheeks in his hands and pulls me closer to him.

He moves one hand, so it slips under the material of my thong. His fingers explore me for a moment before slipping two fingers deep inside of my entrance. I gasp at the sensation, feeling electricity shoot through my veins. A moan escapes past my lips as I rock against him in response, pushing myself up and down onto his fingers.

"Fuck," I hiss as he inserts a third finger. His fingers move in a steady pattern, expertly massaging and caressing in a tantalizing rhythm that makes me lose control. I lift my hips higher and push myself down faster and harder, allowing the pleasure to build. My muscles tense with anticipation as I grind down onto him and bury my face in the crook of his neck. With a scream muffled against his skin, I surrender to the orgasmic bliss cascading through my veins.

Cradling me in his muscular arms, he carries me to the edge of the pool, placing me gently on the lip. His gaze burns with intensity as he slides my bikini bottoms down my legs.

In a raspy whisper, he says "I'm not done with you yet."

CHAPTER 2 - ROWAN

Passion courses through me as I spread Adriana's legs wide, my heart racing as I take in the sight before me. Her beautiful bare pink pussy glistening in the moonlight has me panting from desire. "God, you're gorgeous," I say breathlessly, before lifting her legs out of the water and placing them over my shoulders.

I press hot kisses along her inner thighs, each one more passionate than the last until I'm tantalizingly close to her trembling wet lips. Her moans become louder as I tease her, her body writhing beneath me in ecstasy.

Adriana's breathing has quickened, and she arches her back with pleasure, crossing her ankles behind my neck. I relish the feeling of being trapped against her slick mound as I move up further.

I blow hot air directly onto her sensitive nub before taking it possessively into my mouth like a French Kiss. My tongue moves faster now, swirling around the bundle of nerves and teasingly pulling away with each pass before coming back to give her more pleasure. Her chest rises and falls with the intensity of the moment, almost as if she cannot get enough air.

Her breathing is ragged and gasp-filled with each lick of my hot, wet tongue. I explore further, pushing my hot wet tongue deep inside her dripping wet pussy as far as it can go, tasting her sweet sugary juices. I glance up to see Adriana propping herself up on her elbows while watching me hungrily devour her delicious pussy. My heart pounds like a jackhammer in my chest.

I moan against her as our eyes meet and she cries out in response, then throws her head back with ecstasy. She grabs my hair tightly and begins to buck and thrust her hips in time with each fuck-stroke of my tongue.

"Fuck, yes baby," she cries out.

That dirty little mouth encourages me to go even faster. I continue to fuck her sweet little pussy with my tongue. As I greedily devour her sweet nectar with fervent desperation, I feel her trembling body against me.

Pressed so close to her, I can barely breathe, but my mouth continues to worship her eagerly. I want to make her cum so hard she's dizzy.

My hands roam up her thighs, cupping her ass with one hand as my thumb caresses her swollen clit with the other. I apply gentle pressure and feel a delightful shudder ripple through her body at the sensation.

"Fuck. Fuck. Fuck." She shrieks out, grabbing onto my head for dear life as she rocks and grinds her gloriously wet pussy against my face.

She gasps between breaths, pushing her hips forward into my face. "Oh God! Right there!"

I respond by pressing my thumb firmly against her clit while thrusting my tongue deep inside of her.

"Shit. Fuck. Oh god. I'm coming." She pants and pushes her hips up against my face as she gasps and moans.

I continue tongue fucking her pussy and working her clit between my fingers, sending wave after wave of pleasure through her. She arches her back and gasps, her body tensing as she writhes against me. Her breaths turn to shudders as I feel her pussy gripping my tongue before an explosive flood of warm liquid shoots across my face, filling my mouth and running down my chin.

Still trembling from the intensity of her orgasm, she lies back exhausted against the pool deck, breathing heavily. "I can't believe I just squirted," she says in amazement, a look of satisfaction now present on her face. "I thought that was a myth."

Flashing her a wicked grin, I say. "You're welcome."

Her breath hitches as she looks up at me with a desperate need radiating from every inch of her body. "Oh my god," she moans, her voice cascading with pleasure. "That was so unbelievably incredible. I can't wait. I need you to fuck me now."

Wrapping her legs around my waist, she begs for me to take her right then and there, desperate for me to show her the intense pleasure only I can give.

Pulling her to me, I kiss her passionately, sucking her soft tongue into my mouth, making her taste herself.

I pull back. "You taste amazing," I say, unable to look away.

She smiles sweetly and runs her tongue along her bottom lip before speaking. "I am pretty sweet, aren't I?"

My cock is straining to be free of my swim trunks, my desire for her so intense that it's almost painful. I want nothing more than to take her right here in the pool, but I don't want her first time to be like that. So I climb out of the pool and place one arm under her back and the other beneath her legs. I scoop her up and carry her into the house and toward my bedroom.

We fall onto my bed in a tangle of limbs. She looks up at me with desire shining in her eyes and I feel my heart racing as she looks me over hungrily.

Heat radiates from her fingertips, and without warning, she slides them down my body. She grabs the waistband of my swim trunks, tugging them off almost roughly. Staring hungrily at my hard cock, she runs a finger along it, making me shudder with pleasure. She caresses it with an experienced touch that sends sparks of pleasure all through me. Then, firmly embracing it with both hands, she strokes up and down at an exquisite pace.

Without warning, she takes me in her luscious mouth, sending waves of energy surging through me from head to toe. Her lips are like velvet as they envelop me totally while expertly working the tip with a perfect suction that has me quivering uncontrollably. The feeling is intense, and I know I won't last much longer.

My breath hitches as her hands encircle my shaft and her tongue whirls around me, driving me mad with pleasure. Each swirl is more intense than the last until I'm so close to the edge of ecstasy, I'm afraid of never coming back.

"Stop," I gasp out through gritted teeth. "If you want me inside you, then stop now."

A smirk appears on her face as she pulls away and I fumble for a condom in a drawer of my bedside table. Before I can even pull it out, she has snatched it from my hand and flung it across the room. She looks up at me with an intensity that sends sparks through my veins.

"I'm on the pill and if you're clean, we don't need this," she says with a wicked grin.

My chest tightens at the thought. I've never done it bareback, and the thought of being this close to her without a barrier is too tempting to resist.

Desperate for her touch, I press my body hard against hers. My lips devour hers hungrily and passionately, with an intensity that sends shivers down my spine. Our tongues dance in a passionate embrace before I trail feverish kisses along her neck and collarbone. My hands wander hungrily over her curves, cupping each perfect breast with reverence. Next, I pull one nipple into my mouth and teasingly twist the other between my fingers. She gasps in pleasure as she throws her head back against the bed sheets, arching her body up towards me.

My rock-hard cock is throbbing with desire as I position myself between her legs, rubbing the tip across her already-drenched pussy. I push in only the tip at first to stretch her out. Our eyes meet and I pause for a moment to look deeply into her eyes. "Tell me if it hurts," I whisper huskily, ready to slow down immediately if need be.

She nods in response before eagerly urging me on with a whisper. "Just get it in me already."

I take a deep breath and make my move, slowly pushing forward inch by inch until I have all 8 inches inside her tight heat, feeling the warmth radiating through my body. Both of us gasp in pleasure.

She groans beneath me, her muscles tensing before relaxing into the sensation. "It doesn't hurt, it feels good," she whispers.

I move slowly at first, pushing in and out in a steady rhythm, relishing the pleasure radiating through both our bodies. But when she wraps her legs around me and meets each thrust with equal passion, I lose control. We become a blur of movement as we build up an intense heat that threatens to ignite us both from within. Sweat runs down our bodies like honey and fuels us further still until we are both panting for more.

I thrust into her with a primal hunger, splitting her in two as I pound her pussy until I feel like I'm going to explode. I let out a moan as I feel her walls gripping down around my cock, tight with pleasure.

"Fuck. Oh, fuck yes," she cries out in response and bucks against me as her pussy grips down hard upon my cock, screaming and moaning loud enough to wake the neighbors.

Her inner walls clamp down around my slick cock like a tight vice grip, coiling and squeezing around it in an almost overwhelming sensation of pleasure. My eyes roll back in ecstasy as I feel every nook and cranny of her insides massaging me like a living glove.

"Fill me up," she commands.

"Fuck," I groan out, unable to take any more. Her command pushes me over the edge. My back arches and my cock pulses as cum shoots out of the tip. It flies into her like a rocket, filling her pussy with my hot, creamy jizz.

I collapse onto her, heat radiating off both our bodies. We lay there for what feels like hours afterwards, just looking deep into each other's eyes until our breathing normalizes again.

"That was incredible," I hiss as I press a hard, passionate kiss on her lips. She collapses into my arms in contentment, and I hold her close while she dozes off into sleep next to me, safe in my arms.

I'm unable to fall asleep right away, though. Thoughts of what just transpired on replay in my mind, realizing what I have done. I have crossed a line - deflowered my best friend's barely legal younger sister, breaking the bro code, and worse, breaking the best friend code.

There is no going back to the way things were before, and the thought leaves me feeling torn.

Did I feel bad that I had gone against my best friend's wishes? Yes. Did I regret what had just happened between Adriana and me? Fuck no, I did not. And I would do it again, and again, and again if it's what she wanted me to do.

CHAPTER 3 - ADRIANA

I groggily open my eyes, my body snuggled up against Rowan's warm body. A delicious aroma of bacon and eggs wafts up from the kitchen, sending panic through my veins. I know it's probably Bella, but I can't be for certain. What if Adam got home early? If he caught me in Rowan's bed, there would be hell to pay. He'd likely strangle Rowan with his bare hands!

My eyes fly open, my heart pounding a wild rhythm against my rib cage. I carefully slip out of the bed, making as little noise as possible, and glance around the room for something to throw over myself. My clothes are still downstairs and the last thing I want is to be caught with no clothing on.

Desperate, I dig through Rowan's drawers until I find a t-shirt that is huge and soft against my skin. The shirt reaches my knees, making me look like an oversized child.

Bella grins from ear to ear as she takes in my disheveled state, wearing nothing but Rowan's shirt.

She places one hand on her hip, swaying her hips playfully while teasing me with her bright blue eyes. "Well... well... well. What do we have here?"

The corners of my mouth twitch upwards into a smile as I descend the staircase to meet her gaze. I can't help but feel like my face is about to split apart because of how hard I am smiling.

"Rowan came home early," I explain.

"I can see that," she chimes in with a wink.

"But why are you here so early, Bella?"

Her laughter fills the air. "Early? It's almost noon."

My mouth drops open in shock. "What? Holy shit! How did that happen?" I shriek.

Bella shrugs her shoulders. "I guess Rowan was comfy to snuggle up against, huh?"

I swallow hard as I reply, "I guess so."

Her eyes sparkle mischievously. "So, how was it?"

I pause for a moment and stare at her. I'm not ready to say any of it out loud.

She raises an eyebrow and gives me a knowing look. "I know you did it. You're wearing his shirt and I'm guessing you don't have a stitch on underneath."

I beam at her. "It was amazing!" I whisper - just as the floorboards groan on the balcony stairwell above us.

We look up and see Rowan standing there wearing nothing but his birthday suit. He steps back inside when he notices Bella.

I smirk at Adriana and run up to join him. As I enter his bedroom, I see he's put on a pair of shorts but is still shirtless.

Embarrassed, he starts to explain, "I saw Bella so I figured I'd better put some clothes on..." He pauses, taking in the sight of me wearing nothing but one of his t-shirts.

He grabs me gently and plants a kiss on my lips. "It looks sexy on you," he murmurs against my mouth.

"Thanks," I reply breathlessly, pulling away from him.

"Hey, you two," Bella shouts up to us. "What happened to your phones?"

I stifle a groan and lean back, away from Rowan. "Umm, I left mine out at the pool. I think," I call down to her.

Rowan runs an agitated hand through his disheveled hair. "Mine got soaked when I fell in the pool yesterday. It's in a bowl of rice."

We make our way downstairs to the kitchen where Bella has already set two plates with scrambled eggs, bacon, and toast on them at the breakfast bar for us.

"Thanks, Bella." Rowan says as he sits down.

I follow suit and study Bella suspiciously before asking, "Why are you cooking breakfast for us, anyway?"

Bella bites her lip nervously, her eyes darting between Rowan and me.

"Bella?" I ask, my gaze narrowed and suspicious.

"Adam called me," she blurts out.

My jaw clenches. "Why did he call you?" I ask.

She takes a step back, both of her hands now on her hips. "Because you wouldn't answer your damn phone last night."

I raise an eyebrow at her questioningly. "And?"

She holds up her hands defensively, panic edging into her voice. "I was totally just kidding. I swear. I had no way of knowing that Rowan was actually home early."

I give her a pointed look, exasperation evident on my face. "Bella, what did you do this time?"

Her attempt at looking innocent fails terribly beneath my scowl as she nervously clears her throat. "Like I said before," she says hastily, "I was totally joking."

My gaze shifts to Rowan—his complexion has gone ashen.

Taking a few deep breaths to calm myself down, I lock eyes with Bella and hiss through clenched teeth, "Bella! Just come out with it already!"

She shrugs, only heightening my aggravation. "I suggested, jokingly I might add, that his hot roommate probably got home early and you and him were... occupied." Her eyebrows raise mischievously.

I shake my head in disbelief, astonished. "Bella!" I huff. "Why in the world would you say something like that to Adam?"

Chewing the inside of her lip, she responds slowly. "I'm not sure. You know how I'm always pushing his buttons? Well ... I knew that for sure would push his buttons and so I said it."

She pauses for a moment, gnawing on her bottom lip. "But I honestly thought he'd know it was a joke because, obviously, Rowan was away on business."

Rowan lets out a sharp breath and replies solemnly, "Except I was actually here, and he tried to call me, didn't he?"

Bella's eyes pop open wide and she nods. "At least twenty times."

Rowan shoves his hands through his hair. "Well, shit."

Bella paces back and forth across the kitchen. "I told him repeatedly that I had been kidding, but he booked an earlier flight, anyway. I didn't think it was that big of a deal until I got here and found you two sleeping snugly in Rowan's bed."

Rowan's eyes widen with alarm, and he hisses through gritted teeth, "When was his flight getting in?"

She takes a big breath. "He could be home any minute now."

My heart leaps into my throat and I jump off the bar stool, not even having the appetite for breakfast anymore.

"Don't worry," Bella assures us. "I already tidied up out at the pool. I put the bikini in the guest room, Adriana, and I washed the wine glasses and took out the garbage."

"I need to take a shower," Rowan says.

I contemplate our next move. I need to shower too, but I'm more concerned about cleaning up the place. If worse comes to worse, I can always jump into the pool. So, while Rowan showers, Bella helps me change the sheets on his bed.

Her eyes widen as she takes in the state of Rowan's bed. "Wow, you really did lose your v-card," she says knowingly.

My heart races as I take a deep breath before recounting the events of the night before. I bite my lip. My heart is hammering in my chest.

"Well, spill it," Bella says eagerly.

"Um." I stammer. We tell each other everything, yet here I am struggling with what I have to say. She's no stranger to romance and is always so open with me, so why am I finding it so hard to form these simple words?

"It was..." I stammer, my palms growing sweaty. I struggle to find the right words to describe the passion I felt. "Incredible," I eventually say, my voice barely above a whisper as the memory floods back into my mind. "Beyond anything I've ever felt before."

She nods knowingly and draws closer to me, her hand resting gently on my arm. "Then what's the problem? I mean, other than your brother?" She stares deeply into my eyes, as if willing me to open up and tell her more.

Taking a shaky breath, I let my eyes drift away, trying to avoid her piercing gaze. I can't deny that I want so much more with Rowan, but he also is my brother's best friend. I don't care about that, but Rowan does. There is no way he will want a relationship with me, but I can't help the way my heart aches when I look at him.

"The problem," I whisper, "is that I have god-damned feelings for him and now that he's blown my mind with that sinful mouth and body of his, I'm never getting over him."

Bella raises an eyebrow at me, a smile playing at the corner of her lips. "I wouldn't worry about it. Seems to me he has plenty of feelings for you, too."

"I doubt that," I say, "But he did try to stop me, you know. Said he didn't want me to regret it."

She raises an eyebrow. "How did you convince him?"

Swallowing hard, I look away. "I told him it was just sex."

CHAPTER 4 - ROWAN

I'm out on the patio just waiting for the shit to hit the fan. Adam would be home any time.

Glancing at the pool, I think about last night. I remember Adriana's soft skin beneath my fingers, her delicate curves illuminated by moonlight. Her moans spurring me on as my tongue explored every inch of her body, making her cum so hard she squirted.

I had never elicited such a response from a woman before. And that I did it with my mouth and my tongue makes me feel fairly accomplished considering my limited experience in the oral department. I'd tried it a couple of times years ago and didn't really enjoy doing it. Last night with Adriana was different, though. I could go down on her every day and never tire of it.

I think back to when I found out the trip got cut short and I tell myself it's time that I'm brutally honest with myself and stop the bullshit. I purposefully cut my trip short to come home and seek out Adriana. The hotel room had been paid for, but I had to see her. Last night was exactly what I'd been hoping would happen, despite knowing how wrong it was.

Adriana was just a kid when I met Adam at college, and I had never even met her in person until a year ago. When I first moved here, there had been a housewarming party and Adam's family had invited their friends and family.

As soon as I saw her, a lightning bolt of attraction surged through me. Adriana was like an angel, but with an edge that left my heart fluttering. Our conversation felt effortless and as if the universe had brought us together at that exact moment. Never before had I felt so drawn to another person.

My preconceived notions about Adriana, based on Adam's descriptions of her, had prepared me for the absolute worst. To my utter surprise, though, she was an incredibly mature young adult. When I suddenly realized that the angel I had been so taken by at the party was really his little sister, I felt like I'd been punched in the stomach. She was my best friend's little sister, and she was only 17. Off-limits to me in all ways—mentally, physically, emotionally—I put all my energy into avoiding her. The moment came when I couldn't fight it anymore.

Now, she's getting ready to start college. She's staying in state and attending the university in the next town over. But I can't help but feel guilty. I'm ten years older than her and have had my college experience. Was it wrong of me to develop feelings for someone who was still so young?

I had no choice, though; these feelings were like wildfire in my chest, and Adriana had become the source of them all. And after last night? It was all I could do to keep from throwing myself at her feet. I would do anything for Adriana. Of course, that also meant letting her go if that's what she wanted. It would rip me apart, but I would do it.

Adriana takes my hand in hers and squeezes reassuringly as we sit outside, trying to figure out what to tell Adam.

"We don't have to tell Adam anything," she says.

I sigh. "He's my best friend." I drop my head and stare at the ground, feeling overwhelmed. "It's one thing to just not tell him anything. It's another if he asks me outright if I slept with you and lie to his face."

Suddenly, a warm hand on my shoulder draws my attention back to her. "I get it," she says softly, her eyes gentle and understanding. "I feel the same way. So, if you would rather tell him and get it over with, I'm fine with that too."

I furrow my brow in disbelief. "You are?"

She nods. "My main concern is that if he finds out later, he'll feel like he's lost your trust and that could ruin your friendship for good. If you are honest with him up front, then there's a chance it won't."

My shoulders stiffen at her words. How am I supposed to tell him? I mean, this isn't some casual conversation we are about to have; I was about to drop a bombshell on him that could destroy our friendship in one fell swoop. My stomach churns as I try to make sense of what to do next.

A car pulling into the driveway jolts us both back to reality. Panic races through me as I try to decide what to do next. My heart pounds in my chest like a hammer trying to break free.

Adriana and I exchange nervous glances. "Let's just wait out here and when he comes to talk to us, we'll tell him together," I say, finally finding my voice after what feels like an eternity. Adriana nods in agreement and we wait for another twenty minutes, but neither he nor Bella appear. Our time has run out, it's now or never.

"I can't stand waiting anymore." I grumble, and Adriana takes my hand, her small fingers squeezing my own nervously.

The kitchen is empty, but I spot Adam's suitcase in the corner. Adriana follows me in, her eyes wide with curiosity when we don't see any sign of Bella or Adam.

Suddenly, we hear moaning coming from the upstairs bedroom, along with a few grunts and plenty of bed banging against the wall. My jaw drops open. "No way," I breathe out in disbelief.

"Way." Adriana giggles.

"Holy fucking shit," I whisper, grabbing Adriana's hand and leading her back out to the patio.

Once outside, I give Adriana a sidelong glance. "Did you know about this?"

"That Bella has wanted to get into his pants? Yeah." Her grin grows mischievous as she adds,

"That she was going to do something about it? No clue."

An amused smirk crosses my face. "You know, I think I'm starting to really like your friend, Bella."

"Yeah, she's the best." Adriana says. "But don't get your hopes up about double dates or anything. Bella is only blowing off steam. She likes her boy toys."

The corner of my mouth quirks up and my eyebrow rises skeptically. "Is that what I am?"

She doubles over in laughter. "What? A boy toy?"

I nod.

"You're most certainly not a boy and I like you too much for that," she says.

My heart hammers in my chest as I look into Adriana's eyes and hear her words. "You do?"

She nods. "Yeah. I have since the night I met you."

She drops her gaze. "You don't have to reciprocate. After all, I did tell you it was just sex."

I cup her chin in my hand and tilt it upward, looking deep into her eyes. I can see a slight tremble in her lips. "It wasn't just sex to me." I whisper.

And then, with my heart pounding in my chest, I crush my mouth to hers. Her lips tremble slightly, prompting me to lean down and capture them with mine. Her hands wind around my neck, clinging on as if she never wants to let go of me again.

Our lips eventually part, leaving us both breathless, and Adriana peers up at me with a beaming smile.

"So," she says softly. "Are we together now or what?"

I nod and wrap my arm around her waist, pulling her closer to me. "Yes," I say simply. "Yes, we are."

We both smile and I dip my head to kiss her again, this time more passionately. Adriana runs her hands through my hair as I deepen the kiss and I know that this is the start of something special.

CHAPTER 5 - ADRIANA

After Adam's rendezvous with Bella, he has no room to talk about Rowan and me.

He tries nonetheless, voicing all his objections: "You're too young. You've still got college. For god's sake, he's my best friend."

Adam tries everything to make me feel guilty about my decision, but nothing can change my mind about how I feel about Rowan. So, in an act of desperation, he brings our mother into the discussion. Not that I want to talk to my mom about my sex life, ever. But I do feel that if anyone should tell her anything, it should be me. But over Sunday brunch, Adam takes it upon himself to tattletale to mom that I lost my v-card to Rowan.

Talk about embarrassing! I sink down in my chair, wishing the ground would swallow me whole. But it totally bites him in the ass when instead of lecturing me like Adam expects. She shrugs her shoulders and says, "Well, your sister is a grown up now and can decide who she wants to sleep with."

Adam starts huffing and puffing about it so she adds, "You should be thankful that it was Rowan, someone she could trust, as opposed to some random guy she met up with."

My face breaks out into a smug smile. I quickly take this chance to get my own dig in at Adam for his deplorable behavior and blurt out, "Adam slept with Bella!" I can't help myself and stick my tongue out at him like an impudent child before storming out the door.

***

2 years later...

Rowan and I are still seeing each other. Adam and Rowan have settled their differences and remain close friends and roommates. I think mom's perspective helped to win Adam over. He still gives Rowan a hard time about me sometimes, but it's mostly in good nature. Ultimately, Adam's come to accept that our relationship is different now that I'm an adult.

My college friends are often out at the clubs, chugging drinks, and dancing until the early morning hours, while I opt to spend my time with Rowan instead. After hearing their tales of wild nights and wanting to forget some of the names they'd collected from various hook-ups, I don't feel like I'm missing out on anything. I'm truly thankful that I have Rowan.

I've just completed my last final, and Rowan and I are out to dinner to celebrate completing my sophomore year of college.

"I can't believe you got reservations for this place!" I say, looking around at the upscale restaurant from our corner booth. The soft candlelight glints off the sparkling crystal chandeliers and shimmering wine glasses. A small jazz band is playing a slow and sultry melody at the entrance, creating an atmosphere of sophistication and class.

"The owner owed me a favor," Rowan says, winking at me with that mischievous twinkle in his eye.

"Still, this is way too nice," I take a breath, "and too expensive to just be celebrating the end of finals."

The waitstaff brings us a bottle of vintage wine, and Rowen pours me a glass. He raises his own glass with a smile that reaches his eyes. "And now we can finally celebrate you turning 21 by sharing a bottle at dinner."

My cheeks flush as I feel warmth spread through me. "You already spoiled me rotten for my birthday," I say, taking a sip of the smooth, sweet wine. The rim of the cold champagne glass is cool and slick on my fingertips.

He turns to me and takes my hands in his. His touch is warm and gentle; his gaze is full of admiration and love. He whispers, "Adriana, you're so special."

My heart leaps at the sound of my name on his lips. My stomach somersaults as desire radiates through every fiber of my being.

"Do me a favor and look inside your purse."

I tentatively reach for my purse, which is resting on the seat next to me, and give him a questioning look. He nods encouragingly, and I hesitate before unzipping it to find a small, neatly wrapped box with a pink bow adorning the top.

"You bought me a present?" I gasp.

He nods.

"And you snuck it into my purse?"

He smirks. "Open it."

I stare at it for a moment before looking up to meet his gaze, my heart pounding with anticipation as I pull the box free from my bag. My hands trembling slightly, I carefully peel away the tissue paper to reveal a cardboard box inside. I open it with cautious optimism — only to find a velvet jewelry box nestled inside.

My heart pounds in my chest. Is this what I think it is?

With shaking hands, I pull the tiny box from its larger container and peer over at Rowan, whose grin is so wide I think his face might crack.

He sets the box to the side and takes my shaking hands in his. "Don't you want to know what's inside?"

I nod, giving his hand an anxious squeeze. "Will you open it? I'm shaking too much."

"Adriana, I love you so much. And I'm not saying it has to be any time soon. I'll wait as long as you want. Or, if you want it to be soon, that's okay too. I mean ...,"

I interrupt him. "Rowan, just open the box."

Rowan's face softens, and he releases my hands to lift the lid of the jewelry box slowly. He smiles warmly as he reveals a stunning diamond ring. Glancing up from the sparking gemstone to meet my eyes once more, he asked softly, "Adriana, will you marry me?"

A single tear escapes down my cheek as I nod eagerly in response. "Yes, yes, of course I will!"

Rowan's hands tremble as he gently places the sparkling diamond ring on my finger, and I blink the tears out of my eyes. "Rowan, I love you for saying you'll wait. But I'll marry you tomorrow if you want me to."

His mouth drops open slightly in shock. "Really?"

I beam. "Yes. I would."

The hope and excitement are palpable as Rowan's face lights up in anticipation. "How about this summer?"

A sudden and overwhelming idea strikes me like lightning. "Rowan," I whisper frantically, my eyes blazing in anticipation, "let's get married in your backyard, by the pool!" After all, it was there that our love story began.

His face lights up with joy as he locks his gaze onto mine, searching for confirmation that this is really happening. When our eyes meet and he sees the certainty within them, a wild grin spreads across his lips before he crashes into me with a feverish kiss, sealing our engagement.

***

Get a free short story when you sign up for my newsletter. Sign up here**https://dl.bookfunne l.com/a2samtzbqf**

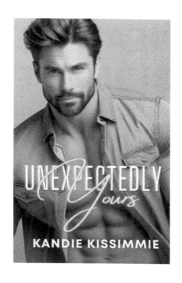

SNEAK PEEK: FORBIDDEN FRUIT

Eden

I'm inside the barn, engaged in a one-sided conversation with Misty, the horse, when I hear an unexpected noise. I think it's Momma or the Reverend. But when I look up to greet them, a stranger stands there instead.

Goosebumps prickle along the back of my neck and I go slack jaw.

Momma raised me right, with manners. She taught me that it's impolite to stare, but I can't help it. He's so beautiful and I've never seen him around here before.

The light filtering in through the barn door illuminates him making him look otherworldly.

Be not forgetful to entertain strangers, for thereby some have entertained angels unawares. That's what the Bible says right there in Hebrews 13, chapter 2.

He can't really be an angel. Or can he?

I must look scared because before I know what's happening the handsome stranger is walking toward me and he says, "Don't be afraid. "

That's when my knees go weak, and I forget to breathe. Because that's what angels always say in the Bible. Am I seriously having a divine encounter with an angel in the barn?

I continue to stare and am now leaning against Misty's stall door, so I don't fall over. Then he speaks again. "I'm Gabriel."

I'm not just having an encounter. This is a transcendent experience with an archangel. I don't know what I've done to deserve such a gift but thank you Jesus.

I feel like I'm fading and realize that I'm still not breathing. I'm losing my balance and falling away from the door. The next thing I know, Gabriel has me cradled in his arms.

I close my eyes and take a deep breath of the best fragrance I've ever smelled in my entire life. Rich, warm, and heady scents of earthy cedarwood and dark vanilla fill me with longing, as if I am desperate for something I can't quite recall.

His strong arms continue to hold me steady and I'm leaning into him. He's stroking my hair. "Are you okay?"

I don't answer because that's when something happens that has me wanting to hold on tighter while simultaneously wanting to run away. My breasts feel tight against my bra, like my nipples could poke right through. There's a heat between my legs accompanied by a tingling feeling that's radiating outward towards all my extremities. My heart pounds in my chest and my breathing picks u p.

I know what's happening to my body. Sort of. Last year, before he moved away, I would sneak behind the baptismal with this boy at church named Adam. When our hands touched or when we kissed similar things would happen to my body. But those sensations were nothing compared to these. Momma and the Reverend would have had a conniption if they'd found out I was kissing a boy. They had forbidden me to date until I was eighteen. Which I am now.

"Are you alright?" He asks again.

I suck in a breath and open my eyes. His golden eyes sparkle as they stare into mine. It's almost like I can see into his soul. And I swear, I don't know what in the world comes over me. I've never even thought of doing something like this. I didn't even know I was capable.

But I press my body right up to his, feeling the firm muscles under his shirt. I can feel every hard inch of him throbbing against me through his jeans too. Something makes me want to climb him like a tree.

Lord, I don't know what's gotten into me. I throw my arms around his neck and then my legs around his waist. It's like I'm moving automatically, not even thinking things through. My lips press up to his and a jolt of electricity travels all the way down my body, pulsing at that place in between my legs where I'm already aching.

He kisses me back and it's nothing like the kisses Adam and I used to share. Especially when he has me pressed tight between him and the wooden partition. The bulge under his jeans presses into the apex of my legs that's now throbbing and tingling.

I've never felt anything so divine. Something tugs at my consciousness with that thought. Divine. I had thought at first he was an angel. It can't be. An angel wouldn't be doing *this* with me. Unless ...

My eyes pop open and I pull my mouth away. I slide down to my feet and smooth my dress.

Satan was an angel once. Technically still is. Fallen angels *would* do something like this.

I take off running as fast as I can towards the house and once inside, I lock all the doors and then go up into my bedroom in the attic.

Sitting on my bed I pull my knees up to my chest. I feel dizzy and lay my head down on my knees.

God allowed a fallen angel to tempt me, and I failed.

After taking a few deep breaths and wiping the tears that had begun falling away, I kneel on the floor and fold my hands in prayer on my bed.

"God please forgive me for giving into temptation."

Then, the memory of the barn flashes into my mind's eye and my body betrays me by feeling all the same sensations it felt before.

I finish my prayer. "God please help me, Amen."

***

Gabriel

Fluttery sensations attack my chest and I lean against the stall door. "Fuck," I swear under my breath and shake my head.

What in the actual hell just happened?

Why was there a beautiful girl in the barn? Why did she kiss me? Or did I kiss her, and she kissed me back? It was all such a blur. I don't know what happened.

One minute I'm standing there and the next she's falling over and I'm catching her. Then our bodies were entwined, and we were making out.

My heart thumps in my chest and my dick pulses.

I let out a breath. "Damn it."

I really need to get this boner under control before the Reverend gets home. Not to mention, I need to get my vocabulary under control. The Reverend doesn't allow cursing in his house, and I am determined to respect his rules as long as I'm visiting.

God she's beautiful, though. I've all but given up on finding a romantic partner. But wouldn't it be crazy if I came back here after all this time and of all the places in the damned world, I found my soul mate here?

Soul mate? Where the hell did that come from?

I've never felt sparks like that with anyone. You hear people talk about chemistry between people and I had all but decided it was a made-up thing. But what just happened between us? That's made a believer out of me. Then there's her eyes. When I looked into the sparkly green depths, I felt as if I could see into her soul. And there's that fluttering feeling back.

So, soul mate ... it could happen, right? Maybe divine intervention or something? Or maybe the Universe decided that I've made enough progress with my problems and coming home to see my dad somehow has tipped the scales in my favor.

She did seem a bit younger than me. But honestly, around here, that wouldn't be all that uncommon. Apparently, she liked what she saw too. But she had run off. It was like she had a sudden realization and then she just ran back to the house leaving me here with all these damned emotions and physical sensations to go along with them.

She could have realized that the Reverend could be home any minute and would find us like that. That would be enough to make me run back to the house, even now, to tell you the truth.

Or maybe she realized something else? The Reverend remarried several years ago. I didn't attend the wedding, of course. She had a daughter named Eden. I remember her from church when she was little. In my mind she's still six or seven years old. She had long dark hair and green eyes.

I run my fingers through my hair and squeeze my eyes shut. Quickly doing the math. Eden? Could it have been? Of course, she would be grown now. I say a quick prayer of please God let her be eighteen.

I'm a grown man, a good twelve years older than her. I should feel ashamed of myself for letting that happen. It really did feel mutual, though. Surely, she's old enough to decide for herself whom she wants to kiss. Or even who she wants to be with?

I take a breath and let it out. Opening my eyes, I plop my head back against the nearby post. Not in the Reverend's household. He would probably pop a vein in his head if he found out what had just happened between Eden and me.

To make matters worse, here I am, coming home to make amends with him after so many years, and I do something so irresponsible. The

Reverend would spin it into something dirty and sinful on top of it all.

Then reality slaps me in the face. All those things would be perceived badly by the Reverend. Very badly. But this one is the icing on the cake.

I just kissed my stepsister.

It's like a miracle and a damnation all at once. Suddenly I feel like the Reverend and God are conspiring against me.

To continue reading order Here: https://linkt r.ee/kandiekissimmie

Twelve years since he last stepped foot in Paradise Falls, Gabriel returns with hopes of reconciling with his estranged father, the Reverend.

But upon his return, Gabriel discovers an irresistible temptation - Eden, his innocent stepsister. With a love as forbidden as the fruit itself, will Gabriel succumb to his desires, or will he be able to keep away from this forbidden love?

Forbidden Fruit is a Short & Steamy Age-Gap Contemporary Romance. It's a standalone with no cliff hangers and a Happily Ever After. It's about a 3-hour read, so if you like a smoking hot quickie, then this book is for you!

Order Here: https://linktr.ee/kandiekissimmie

*Or visit my linktree: https://linktr.ee/kandiek issimmie

A NOTE FROM KANDIE

Hi, thanks for reading House-sitter Virgin. I hope you enjoyed reading about Adriana & Rowan as much as I enjoyed writing about them. If you can't get enough of age-gap romance with a happily ever after, then you might like one of my other short & steamy reads:

- Forbidden Fruit: A Hot Age-Gap Contemporary Romance

- Babysitter Seduction: A Short & Steamy Age Gap Romance with Her Boss

- Unexpected Miracle: A Short & Steamy Single Dad Age-Gap Romance

- Breaking His Rules: A Hot Age-Gap Romance with Her Boss

I also enjoy writing the forbidden stepsibling trope. If you like this trope, then you might also like one of these short & steamy reads:

- Stepbrother Seduction: Short & Steamy Stepbrother Taboo Erotica

- Stepsister's Joyride: Steamy Stepbrother Taboo Erotica

- Stepsister Secret: Short & Steamy Stepsister Taboo Erotica

- Midnight Possession: A Stepbrother's Forbidden Halloween Romance (Midnight Masquerade)

- Midnight Obedience: A Hot MFMM Halloween Menage (Midnight Masquerade)

All of my books can be accessed with the following link:

https://linktr.ee/kandiekissimmie

ABOUT THE AUTHOR

Hi, I'm Kandie. I live in the Midwest and I write short & spicy HEA Romance & Taboo Erotica. My books range from 5000 words on the short end to 50K on the long end. I don't like closed doors, cliffhangers, or sad endings and so you find those in my books. What you will find is plenty of heat along with a little bit of sweet.

I adore writing age-gap romance, hot single Daddies, and step-siblings.

If you're looking for a short & spicy read to heat

up your nights or to feed the flames of your imagination, make sure to check out my work!

If you enjoy my spicy stories, please consider leaving a rating and/or review on Goodreads.

Find me on Instagram and Facebook

Links to my books, Goodreads, and social media can be found at the following link:

https://linktr.ee/kandiekissimmie

BOOK BLURB

What's this book about?

Staying away from Adriana has been my mission for months. The desire that stirred in me for her was wrong on so many levels.

But when I come home earlier than expected from my business trip and find the goddess sunning at my pool, all my promises to myself fly out the window.

- I forget she's only eighteen.

- I forget she's my best friend's little sister.

- I forget Adam would surely kill me if anything were to happen between us.

This is a complete short romance story (around 7500 words), and contains hot, sensuous, explicit love scenes. It's a stand-alone tale with no cliffhanger and it has an HEA ending. It is meant for ages 18+. Enjoy!

9 798223 398301